ECHOES OF THE /
BY GELINEAU AI

A Reaper of S
Rend the Da.
Best Left in the Shadows
Faith and Moonlight
Broken Banners (coming soon)

PRAISE FOR A REAPER OF STONE

"Gelineau and King have created a multi-layered world which resounds with... traditional fantasy yet unfolds in the fast-paced and action-filled narrative which we've come to expect... [they] have fashioned a universe I would wish to return to time and time again."

– *Books by Proxy*

"A classic fantasy tale with a strong, admirable heroine and a nice emotional punch. Great start to an enjoyable new series!"

– RL King, author of *The Alastair Stone Chronicles*

"[T]he myths and legends are tangible and the world's history lingers just beneath the surface of the storyline. I loved the resolution."

– *Galleywampus*

"I don't know if you can call a book lovely, but *A Reaper of Stone* as a fantasy has a lovely quality to it."

– *White Sky Project*

"I would recommend this instant classic to young adults and seasoned fantasy lovers alike."

– Patrick McQueen, *President, CWC South Bay Writers*

MARK GELINEAU
JOE KING

A REAPER OF STONE

AN ECHO OF THE ASCENDED

First Printing: September 2015

v4.2

Gelineau and King

ISBN 978-1-944015-01-5

www.gelineauandking.com

ACKNOWLEDGMENTS

Mark: A huge thank you to my dad, Dan Gelineau, my brother Dave, my wife Tiffany, and my son Bryce for their love and devotion. And to my mom, Pam Gelineau, who I miss every day.

Joe: To Irene, Emma, and Kate. Thank you. You guys make me a better everything.

A massive thanks to the team that helped put it all together:
Jason, TJ, Vikki, Young, Marija, and Alisha.

And also to our friends and beta readers:
Jason, Dave G, Emily, David C, Maria, Maggie, and Samantha.

This book is dedicated to my mother, Pam Gelineau,
whose legacy of love, care and devotion will never stop
being a constant source of inspiration and strength.

I miss you, Ma.

And I know you would have been a fan of Elinor.

PROLOGUE

Conbert's hands were slick with sweat on the reins, despite the cold breeze. Every rustle of the long yellow grass, every whistle of the wind, any sound not the rhythmic clop of his horse's hooves on the worn cobblestone road sent his eyes darting and heart racing.

He had traveled the Reach Road two times previous. Each time had been without incident. Each time, he had arrived at his destination hale and whole, without even a glimpse of the fabled predators the grasslands were so famous for. Yet each time, the sense of dread, of cold fear, had been with him.

The first time, he had tried to play the part of the brave hero, riding forth on a grand quest like the legendary figures in the old stories. That lasted until he caught sight of the infamous drowning grass. The blades were the height of a man and they moved with a sinuous and lifelike grace on each side of the wide stone road.

The fear had started then, shattering whatever myth he might have fabricated of Conbert Eylnen, the future valiant officer of the King's Own. In the face of that grass and what he knew could be hiding under it, he was just Con, apprentice engineer and architect, student of the academy, and anxious to get the hell out of there.

Somewhere far out across the sea of grass, a lone tree rose up like an island. It marked the halfway point in crossing the grassland. It had often given Con comfort. But this time, beneath the shade of its heavy, twisted boughs, there was movement.

A human shape.

Impossible. The only road through the drowning grass was the one he was on now. No one would be stupid enough to travel into the middle of the cursed grass, set up like a picnic for the rendworms.

Con pulled his horse to a halt. Reaching down to the heavy saddlebag, he pulled out his surveyor's glass and raised the delicate instrument to his eye.

Sure enough, there was a person. A girl. She seemed tall, but even with the glass, it was difficult to judge at this distance. She had short, blonde hair that was almost white as it ruffled in the wind. What really caught his attention was her clothing: the familiar grays of an academy cadet. The same grays he had worn as an underclassman a year ago.

The fear came back, but this time wild. The girl was doomed, marooned at that tree surely as any castaway on a lost island. It was only a matter of time until the rendworms caught wind of her.

Before he knew what he was doing, Con urged his horse into a gallop, off the stone road and into the undulating grass. His breath rasped and tears blurred his eyes.

From the wind, he thought. Tears because of the wind. Not because I am stupid and going to die out here.

He rode hard across the grassland, the twisted spire of the tree ahead of him. As it drew closer, he saw the cadet had caught sight of him. She waved frantically. Conbert focused on her desperate movements, shoring up his rapidly disappearing courage with the knowledge that he was her only hope.

Something brushed his leg and he almost shrieked, but realized it was only a heavy stalk of grass. The tree and the waving girl were a few lengths away now.

Con leaped from the saddle, stumbled, and fell on his face, but he got up quickly. Breathlessly, he stood before the girl. "It's alright, cadet," he gasped. "I can take you out—"

Her hand shot out, covering his mouth. It was almost too fast to follow and his eyes widened with shock.

The cadet met his gaze with a cold, hard look of her own. There was a focus there and not the desperate gratitude Con had expected. Slowly, she raised her free hand and laid a single finger against her lips.

Utterly confused, he could only nod.

She cocked her head, listening. Tall and fairly thin, she was not a delicate beauty. Her features were too strong, too sharp for that, but her clear, blue eyes were vibrant as she searched the grass around them. She sighed and released the hand over his mouth.

Con drew a deep breath. "Cadet, what are you doing out here?"

The girl turned and then, appearing to notice the black and silver uniform, snapped to a smart salute. "Forgive me, sir. I was hunting a rendworm."

"You're what? Are you absolutely mad, girl?" he asked, his voice rising.

"No, sir. Not at all. I am merely here to honor the First Trial of Aedan," she said, bowing her head momentarily. "I am not to return without the jaw of a rendworm, but so far, none have appeared."

"The First Trial of Aedan?"

Con's eyes grew wider. The Hunt. The joke upperclassmen played on first-year cadets at the Academy. The older students regaled them with stories of the First King, Aedan, and the legend of how he bested a field of colossal rendworms to earn a meeting with an ancient one, the Shepherd of Tree and Stone.

Only there was no Hunt.

It was all an elaborate ruse, a traditional jape each first-year cadet class went through. The cadets were stopped at the gate of the Academy, chased and beaten by older cadets wielding sticks and wearing garish costumes. And then the ale casks were brought out and everyone would get ripping drunk.

No one ever actually went out to hunt the damn things.

He looked at the girl again. For her to be out here meant she must have been very sheltered or very stupid. But that didn't explain why the other cadets wouldn't have stopped her at the gate.

Conbert felt suddenly cold. Had they done this on purpose? Had they sent her unknowingly to her death? The chill turned to anger. The Academy had never been a warm place, but it had never been this cruel.

Conbert opened his mouth to tell the girl the truth about her fool's errand, but saw her posture change. She stood absolutely still, looking past him, a long-handled black mace in one hand. His horse danced skittishly as the grass waved around it.

The girl put a hand on his shoulder. Her voice was low. "Whatever happens next, you mustn't move."

And then the ground underneath the horse exploded and a pale white form the size of a wagon erupted into the air. The horse let out a scream that turned into a wet gurgle as white writhing tentacles enveloped the animal. The copper tang of blood filled the air and Conbert felt his stomach lurch.

He thought to go for the sword at his side, but he saw the girl's eyes.

He held himself still as another of the creatures breached the drowning grass. It was a huge mass of rippling white flesh, except at the front, where the mouth opened like an exposed wound. Massive tearing fangs lined the pink maw, and white tentacles writhed from the worm's throat, seeking the remnants of the thrashing horse. The two monsters tore the horse apart in seconds, powerful tentacles flaying meat from bone with horrific efficiency.

As the rendworms began to slide across the ground in their direction, Con felt a terror urging him to run. He fought against it, trying to focus instead on the perfect stillness of the young girl as the huge worms slid past them.

Then the girl moved.

The young cadet was fast and sure as she darted forward. She struck out with the mace, swinging it with both hands, and smashing it into the rendworm's side. There was a loud crack, and Con knew that somewhere inside the sinuous horror, a bone had broken under the blow.

The rendworm let out a keening screech that stabbed Con's ears and took the breath from his lungs. The injured creature folded its bulk around, trying to round on the girl. The crown of white tentacles snapped and writhed like angry serpents, seeking her.

Instead of retreating, she moved into the circle of the rendworm's turning bulk. The mace carved through the air once more, the flanged head crashing squarely just behind the enormous hooked jaws and tentacles. This time, there was no crack like thunder, but a wet sound like the smashing of rotting fruit. The rendworm immediately shuddered and collapsed to the ground dead.

The other rendworm came now, covering Con with a shower of earth, a massive shadow blocking out the sun. Bringing his blade free of its sheath, he held it before him in desperation as one of the tentacles lashed at him. By some fortune, Con's sword came across his body right in the path of the slashing tooth of the tentacle. Con dropped to the ground as the horror reared for another strike.

There was an explosion of gore as the creature's soft abdomen was crushed under the girl's mace. The white flesh shuddered and collapsed, and Con scrambled away from the new corpse. Through the noxious rendworm blood dripping down his face, he peered at the young cadet.

Her eyes shone with excitement and triumph.

"From the stories, I thought they would be bigger," the girl said, her voice colored in disappointment.

Conbert looked at her, unable to stop shaking, unable to keep from staring as she handed him a water flask. She walked to the first corpse and began working away at the creature with the short blade from her belt. With quick, sure movements, she tore free the huge serrated jaws of the rendworm.

The girl grinned ear to ear. "They have no eyes, but they can feel your vibrations when you move. You did incredibly well, sir."

Con could only nod dumbly. Finally, he found his tongue. "Conbert Eylnen," he said, unsure of what else to say. "My name is Con."

The cadet nodded as she tore out the jaw of the second rendworm. "Elinor," she said, handing him the bloody mandible. "That one's yours, but I think we had better get on our way before we attract any more attention. Don't you agree?"

Con shook his head in disbelief. "After you," he finally managed.

Elinor smiled and started for the road.

Con made sure to follow close behind.

A REAPER OF STONE

AN ECHO OF THE ASCENDED

ACT 1

The rain came down heavily. The torrent filtered through branches, reducing it to fat drops that beat an irregular staccato on the solid-steel pauldron over Elinor's left shoulder. Her short blonde hair was tucked inside the hood of an oilskin cloak.

Trees rattled with the heavy patter of rain, but the sound was hard for her to discern, lost amidst the jingle of tack and rattle of wagons carrying engineers and their equipment. Coarse laughter and grumbling from work crews echoed down the column of wagons as they marched through the mud.

Beyond them, the caravan swelled with attendants and toadies of Lord Piersym. Bright colors and gaudy fabric, now stained with mud, made it look more like a bedraggled circus troupe than a lord's entourage. The sight of it made her already sour mood even worse. It was a reminder of the duty she detested, but had been ordered to perform.

Near the head of the column, Elinor saw Con trying to coordinate the passage of an equipment-laden wagon around a group of horsemen. After some pointed gestures at the riders, Con got the wagon back on its way and then headed back up to Elinor, shaking his head. As he came up, he snapped a sharp salute.

"Lieutenant," he said formally.

"Journeyman Engineer," Elinor said as she returned the salute. "Trouble there, Con?"

"You'd think these people had never been out in the rain before."

"It's the first time most of them have set foot outside of Resa," she said easily.

Crossing his arms, Con smirked. "It rains in the capital too."

"Yes, but there they have all those fine cobbled roads you engineers are always maintaining. No such luxuries out here in the marches."

He shook his head. "It's mud and rain, Elinor. They make out like it's one of the trials of great Aedan himself." He gestured wide with his arms. "And lo, did great Aedan, unifier of man, face the trial of damp clothing and saddle chafing."

Elinor laughed. Somehow, Con always had been able to do that. It had been two years since she had seen him, and she realized how much she missed his company.

Con caught her eye and gave her a lopsided grin. "Is that a smile at last? I was beginning to think I was losing my touch."

Rubbing her horse's neck and sending fat drops of rain flying, Elinor shook her head. "No. It's this place. This duty. Taking down these keeps."

At that, Con's eyes narrowed slightly. "Reaping? I'd thought you'd be happy to clear these old relics of war." As she looked back at him, he shrugged. "Don't get me wrong. I am loathe to destroy such craftsmanship. But if there is no lord to steward them, it's better they come down than fall into the hands of bandits or whatever else might be lurking out here in the marches."

"Well, they wouldn't be abandoned if the lords of the marches didn't spend all their days locked in the capital, gambling on Razor duels, and drinking and whoring the nights away."

The words came out more bitterly than intended, and she saw mild surprise on Con's face, but it shifted to a wry smile. "Well, when you say it like that, you make it sound like no fun at all."

Elinor chuckled. "Present company excluded, of course, Lord Eylnen. You, my friend, are different."

"Damn right," he said, smiling warmly.

The two friends lapsed into silence as they watched the clumsy caravan of hangers-on navigate the mire of the road. At last, Con spoke. "You sure you're alright? I don't remember things like this weighing on you as heavily in the past." He paused. "Of course, I suppose, there were always bigger things to worry about."

She wanted to explain, but found she couldn't put everything into words. "That was a long time ago, Con," she said. "It's different out here in the marches. You'll see." She took a deep breath, forcing the melancholy spirit down and smiled. "But I am glad you are here."

"Me too," Con said.

"We are nearing the keep," Elinor said, nodding ahead. "Now that your engineers are under my command, let's see if we can bring this rag-tag caravan to its destination in some semblance of order."

"I'd rather face the rendworms again," Con said, falling into place beside her. "At least they didn't complain as much."

Elinor headed back to the front of the column, smiling to herself the entire way.

The dense trees of the forest gave way to a rolling plain sloping down into a narrow ravine. In the distance, Last Dawn Keep rose in the shadow of the surrounding cliffs. It was tall and narrow at the base, a square of hard, cold stone with two towers reaching into the sky.

The setting sun was sinking into the mountains, casting the keep into shadow and obscuring the small village at its base. A light flickered to life in the distance, just a tiny glimmer. Then a second and third. One after another, torches flared until the entire road, from the village to the keep, was lined with light. It was a beautiful sight, and one she had never seen before.

Conbert watched silently beside her. She knew he was as loathe to ruin the moment with talk as she herself was. Elinor gave him a quick smile and then urged her horse to the village.

What must have been the entire population of the village stood there. Each person held a torch, flames sputtering and hissing in the rain. They stood silently as Elinor and the column passed, but she knew their eyes were only on her.

They were here to witness the officer of the King's Army, in her somber black and silver, lead the troop of engineers and laborers to the fortified keep that had stood over their homes for generations. The keep where their grandparents and great grandparents had fought and bled for their lord and the land.

The keep that Elinor had been charged with dismantling.

Elinor had seen those faces before. She was used to the looks of sadness and resentment that followed her. They were the same expressions she had found across the kingdom as lords died and their lands were annexed. As she came to destroy a legacy of honor and tradition that she herself admired.

Yet, it had never been like this. Never this procession through the darkness.

It gnawed at her. Pulled at her. Where were the shouts and the curses? Where were the angry threats of violence and retribution? The people had the same look of sadness, but they stood in perfect stillness as she passed.

Before the open gate of the keep, two figures knelt on the stone path. One was an old man in heavy armor, his white hair hanging down lank in the pouring rain. Beside him knelt a young girl, no more than sixteen summers and slight of frame. They wore the blue and gray of the deceased Lady Kian Lliane. Each had a shield placed on the ground before them and their blades were resting across their palms.

Elinor stared open-mouthed. The River of Light. The Offering of Steel. These were ancient traditions performed to welcome esteemed guests to the lands. Gestures of honor long since abandoned in these times. Acts from the storybooks and legends Elinor had studied so intently as a child.

Now she was being honored with them herself.

The old man spoke without raising his head. "I am Aebelm, once First Blade of Timberline. The household of Lady Kian Lliane, blessed daughter of the First Ascended, now lost to this world, welcomes you. We meet you with light in the darkness. We meet you with steel to safeguard you."

Behind her, Elinor heard the creaking of the carriage door opening. "What is that?" Lord Piersym demanded, leaning out of the carriage. He frowned in the heavy rain and ducked back inside. "Yes, yes," he said, and a dismissive hand came out from the curtained window of the carriage. "Have them tend to the horses and such. The sooner I am out of this damned weather, the happier I will be."

Elinor's face fell in disgust at the lord's casual disregard, but Aebelm rose silently and sheathed his blade.

"See to the lord and his party," he said.

The young girl rose to her feet, eyes remaining downcast. She picked up their shields and cleared the path inside. Piersym's party followed her.

Elinor dismounted and walked to the old man.

"Lieutenant," he said, his eyes on her silver pin of rank. "Please go inside out of the rain and join the lord. I will see to your mount."

Elinor slowly drew her own blade and placed it across the palms of her hands. "I walk in the light you provide. I trust your steel in place of my own," she said, finishing the words of the ancient rite of honor the old man had started.

He gave her a sad smile. "I thank you," he said.

The sincerity in his voice shook Elinor to the core. The loss of his liege had hurt this man, but his pride and honor shone in his eyes.

"Come inside, soldier," he said. "Be welcome here in the ancient seat of Timberline."

Elinor inclined her head. "I would be honored," she said, then followed the old warrior into the keep that had once been his home.

ACT 2

The damp air was heavy as Elinor pulled off her cloak and hung it to dry. A door at the far end of the stable glowed with light. Rich, tantalizing smells drifted through, promising warmth and comfort.

The young girl was brushing down her horse and offered Elinor a smile, which she returned. Though young, the girl carried a blade easily. She had had training; that was clear. But the shield on her back was too big for her. It was well cared for, but the surface was marred and pitted with a legacy of battle. The old man, Aebelm, had carried a similar shield, adorned with the same crest.

Elinor extended a hand to the girl. "I'm Elinor."

The young girl clasped forearms with Elinor. "Tae," she said.

"You are a Razor?"

Tae nodded, putting aside the brush.

"You and your... grandfather, Aebelm. You both served Lady Lliane?"

Tae nodded once more, but this time, her eyes fell away. Elinor recognized the weight of grief as it settled onto the girl like a stone as she spoke, "Me, my grandfather, and my father. We all served the lady."

Elinor bowed her head slightly. "Your father was First Blade then. I am sorry for your loss, Tae."

Before the girl could respond, a figure entered through the stable door, rain dripping from the dark maroon leather of his coat. He wore an arrogant sneer on his lean, vulpine face, and his cold eyes locked onto hers. Ephed, First Blade to Lord Piersym.

"Showing up the new lord of this land at the moment of his arrival is a display of startling stupidity," Ephed said. "Even for you."

Elinor swallowed a retort and ignored him.

"Did you not hear me, Reaper?"

He was baiting her, as he had throughout their trek. She did not rise to it though. She turned pointedly back to Tae. "Would you grab my saddlebags for me, Tae?"

Ephed closed the distance and pushed the girl out of the way, causing her to fall into Elinor's horse and making the animal rear slightly. Elinor caught Tae's arm and kept her from falling to the ground.

Elinor rounded on Ephed, the cold blue of her eyes meeting his directly. "I heard you fine, Razor." She eased Tae away and motioned for her to leave. As Tae disappeared around the corner, Elinor kept her eyes on Ephed. "Your lord was offered an honor. Which he refused. I merely accepted in his stead."

"You insulted him." Ephed's lips shifted into a cold smile. His long, dark hair hung over his eyes. He pulled it back, revealing a V-shaped scar on his throat. The Victory Kiss was a testament to how dangerous he was, but Elinor did not need the mark to know that. She could smell it on him; old blood like beaten copper.

"I did not think the great lord of Hearthfire March was so easily insulted. And as for you, Ephed. I had assumed a Razor of the first rank would be able to handle more." She smiled. "I apologize if I underestimated your sensitivities, Razor."

Ephed shook his head, but his cold smile remained. "You have no power here, Reaper. You are merely an accessory. Your pretty uniform, a bit of decoration. It is best you remember your place."

"That's where you're wrong," Elinor said without hesitation. "I am the king's agent. Duly appointed and charged. You and your lord have no power here until after the reclamation ceremony I will preside over. And that is only after I have deemed whether your lord is fit to rule."

Ephed barked with laughter. "Lord Piersym was hand chosen by the warden. The ceremony is merely a formality." He clucked his tongue. "I'm disappointed at how short-sighted you are, Reaper. Soon, Piersym will return to Resa, and I will be in control of both Hearthfire and Timberline in his stead. Lord in all but title of this land and its people. It would be wise not to invoke my terrible wrath, don't you think?"

Elinor knew this man's type well. She had been facing versions of him since she was a child in the orphanage. A bully, flexing his power.

She stared hard into his eyes. "I serve the king and the king's law. I am here to serve my duty and nothing else but that. I am not here to indulge your delusions of nobility. There is a difference between being a great man and playing at one, Razor. If there is a problem between us, let us deal with it now. Otherwise, go play your games somewhere else."

Ephed's face colored red, causing the scar on his neck to stand out in vivid white. His hand went to the hilt of his blade, and an electric charge filled the air, emanating from him. Razors like Ephed were able to draw upon a power from the world around them, and Elinor had seen them use that power to break the very laws of nature. He was touching that power now.

Elinor stood firm, one hand on the hilt of her blade and the other resting on the short-handled mace that hung at her belt. Her eyes were hard as she stared back.

Ephed smiled, and the throbbing hum in the air died away as he let his power slip away. "I have no intention of delaying my lord's ascension to Timberline," he said evenly. "As you say, we must attend to the ceremony. But after..." his voice trailed off and his smile grew even wider. "I am in no rush, Reaper. After all, I plan to be here for a long, long time." With that, he turned and walked away, whistling tunelessly.

Elinor did not move until he had gone completely, and only then did she unclench her jaw and move her hands from her weapons. A sound came from behind her, and she turned to see the girl, Tae, staring at her. Elinor sighed. "You should have left. You're lucky he didn't see you there. That is not a man who would enjoy someone witnessing damage to his pride."

Tae raised her chin. "I am a Razor of the Aegis school, being trained by the greatest fighters in the kingdom."

"You are still a student. Untempered. And he is a Razor of the first rank. More than that, he has ten other Razors under his command as part of his lord's escort. He is not someone to trifle with."

"Or stare down?" Tae said with a hint of a smile.

Elinor shook her head and kept her eyes hard. "Stay out of his sight until the transfer of power is complete. And even after that, Tae. Stay away from that man." Elinor walked toward the warmth and light coming from the kitchen. "That's what I intend to do."

***

Rich warmth enveloped Elinor like a blanket. There was something comfortingly familiar about the kitchen. It immediately brought Elinor back to the orphanage where she had lived. Her shifts under Matron Mother Gytha had been her most cherished in the rotation of chores. Now, that sense of home warmed her more than the heat of the roaring fire.

In the center of the controlled chaos, an older woman directed the flow of things. She held a wooden spoon in one hand and used it to command, like a battlefield marshal. Her iron-gray hair was plaited in a long braid down her back and she wore a faded apron.

Aebelm approached Elinor and motioned her forward as the gray-haired woman turned to regard them. "Aebelm," she said, eyes wide, "what are you doing, leading one of the King's Own through the mess of my kitchen? Forgive my husband's foolishness, Officer. Allow me to show you the way back to the main hall."

"There is no need, Mistress. I am right where I would choose to be."

"Is that right?" said the older woman, looking her over with a bemused smile. "Perhaps my Aebelm is not such the old fool I think him to be."

Aebelm folded his arms over his chest. "As I so often remind you, Bilia," he said in a low rumbling voice.

"Welcome to you," Bilia said, bowing formally low.

Elinor placed a hand over her heart. "I seek to share the light of your fire, in the dark of the night," she said. There was a satisfaction and a sense of rightness to giving voice to words and traditions that had long faded from use in the world.

Bilia stood tall before Elinor. "I offer you the gifts of hospitality. Fire against the darkness of the night. Bread and salt against the ravages of the day. Tales and song against the loneliness of the world."

"I thank you," Elinor said softly.

"You are a rare find for an army officer indeed," Bilia said, pulling out a chair.

Elinor sat down and allowed the warmth of the kitchen to soak into her. Bilia resumed her orchestration of the kitchen, preparing the welcoming feast. She did pause long enough to place a warm hunk of dark bread and a slice of cheese before Elinor, which she accepted with a smile.

She had barely finished her last bite when Aebelm approached her. Tae followed behind, her eyes on Elinor.

Aebelm bowed his head. "I am sure you must be weary from the road, Lieutenant. But before we direct you to your chamber, I was wondering if you might enjoy a tour of Last Dawn Keep?"

There was a formality to his words, but there was also a sense of pride and excitement. Elinor smiled at him. "I would love to," she said, rising to her feet and following them out.

The great hall was still being set. The honored guests had retired to their rooms and servants were preparing for the dinner. Suspended from the high beams of the ceiling were tall banners, their colors faded with age. The soft shadows cast from the hearth made the banners seem to dance. Each bore the crest of one of the First Ascended, the great heroes who stood against the Ruins and other creatures of the Dark to begin the dominion of mankind in Aedaron.

Elinor stared in awe, whispering their names as she looked at each one. The open hand sigil of Garhard. The broken sword of Baheyer. The painted mask of Talan. Finally, the stone crown emblem of Aedan himself. Her words were soft, but they carried in the space of the hall.

Aebelm moved beside her. "Those banners have hung in this hall for as long as my family has been here," he said. "The tale is that the First Ascended themselves placed them there." Elinor looked at him and he shrugged. "I used to scoff at that idea, but as I have grown older, I have come to realize that Timberline and this keep are very old. And things that seem impossible to a young man can become quite real in time."

Elinor raised an eyebrow, wanting him to elaborate further, but the old man moved on. Tae motioned for Elinor to follow.

"If you like that, you will love what is next," the girl said.

Tae led Elinor into a small vestibule. As Elinor entered, she stopped short, her attention riveted by what was before her.

Covering the entire wall of the chamber was a massive tapestry. It towered over her, the bright colors in sharp contrast to the cold, gray stone wall. In beautiful detail, it captured the legend of the First Trial of Aedan. How, in the darkest times for humanity, he had bested a field of rendworms and climbed the highest peak to meet with a god of the old age, the Shepherd of Tree and Stone.

Elinor approached slowly, taking in the sheer expanse of it. She walked down the length of the woven fabric, her fingertips lightly touching it as she moved. As she did, the words of the old tale came unbidden to her lips.

"And the Shepherd of Tree and Stone took Aedan to the tallest peak, where he looked across the darkness and saw the fires of the tribes of man," she intoned. "Each was a lonely light flickering in isolation, the dark pressing in to extinguish such defiance. A thousand fires in the night. Separated. Alone. So close to one another and yet so far. And Aedan wept for his people. Not for what they were. But for what he knew they could become. A great fire to drive back the darkness."

She pulled her hand away from the tapestry and wiped at the tears in her eyes. She looked over to Tae and Aebelm. "I'm sorry," she said with an embarrassed laugh. "When I was a child in the orphanage, my friends and I would play the roles of these heroes. We would recite these stories to each other." She shook her head. "They made us feel like we were more than just orphans. Like we were destined for great things." Elinor laughed and dried her eyes once more. "It was a long time ago."

"There is nothing to apologize for," Aebelm said solemnly. "Such reverence for the old ways is nothing to be ashamed of."

His words touched Elinor, but it also made it all the more important she say what she needed to say next. "I am grateful to have seen what you are showing. And I understand what you are doing and why you are doing it. This place is special. It is a monument to a time of honor and glory. Things that I treasure as well. But I cannot be swayed from my duty. I am sorry, but the keep must fall."

The old man and his granddaughter exchanged a look that Elinor could not quite figure out, and then Aebelm shook his head. "You are a loyal servant of the king. Something that is all too rare in these times. And duty is something that we in Timberline understand intimately, Lieutenant. If the keep must fall, then so be it."

Aebelm moved closer, his voice lowering. "But it is not the keep itself that is sacred. It is what it was built to protect that is truly sacred. And not only to Timberline, but to all of Aedaron." His narrowed eyes held her and Elinor could not look away. "That is why Timberline must not go to the hands of a man like Piersym."

The clouds of her confusion parted, and her sense for danger, that part of her that always seemed to know exactly when things were about to go wrong, went heavy with dread.

It was Tae who stepped forward now, her wide eyes shining. "Piersym has long desired Timberline. He seeks it for the wealth he can wring from the forests, ignorant of the true treasure of this land. When he learned that the Lady was to be married, he... he struck." As she spoke, her composure began to crack.

"Married?" Elinor said. Looking from the girl to her grandfather, it suddenly made sense. "Your father. The First Blade. That was who the Lady Lliane was to marry?"

"They did marry!" Tae hissed. "In the old way, with the spirit of the forest as their witness."

Aebelm nodded. "My granddaughter speaks the truth. By right, Tae is the rightful heir to Timberline March. As you said, Lieutenant. Your duty is to the king, and as the King's Reaper your task is to ensure the line is ended and usher in the new lord." He raised his chin in a gesture of defiant pride. "My lady's line is not ended. It lives, here, with my granddaughter. And you, Lieutenant, have the power to ratify her claim and keep the march out of Piersym's grasp."

"Stop!" Elinor said, her voice cracking through the empty room. "Stop and listen very carefully to what I say. Piersym is many things, but he is no fool. He has come here with ten Razors and that vicious bastard, Ephed. At even the merest hint of rebellion, those dogs will be released from their chains and they will kill anyone who is even remotely an inconvenience."

"We are telling the truth, Elinor!" Tae said.

"The truth will not keep you alive, girl. It could not save your father." Almost immediately, Elinor regretted her harsh words, seeing the impact of them on the girl. But she did not hold back. These two had to know that what they were considering was utter madness. "The old ways of honor are not made for a world where men like Ephed and Piersym hold power," she said bitterly.

Tae bristled at her words, but Elinor continued, not allowing either the girl or Aebelm a chance to speak. "There are wolves in your home. You must keep that in mind before you speak. Speak no more of this to anyone. Let this pass. This is not a fight you can hope to win."

With that, she turned and walked from the room. All the comfort and magic of the place was gone, replaced with cold dread. New world or old, it seemed the stain of treachery and the promise of violence was always near. She just hoped the old man and the girl were smart enough to avoid running headlong into it.

ACT 3

The sun rose, bathing Last Dawn Keep with warm, orange light. Elinor watched the sunrise from her window. She had been up for hours, last night's events weighing heavily on her mind.

The familiar sound of metal on stone rang across the ravine. Con, it seemed, was wasting no time getting things going. There would be no sleeping in for anyone in Last Dawn Keep.

Elinor dressed quickly. She washed her face in a basin of cold water, then left her chamber, walking down the halls with a quick step.

She found Con at the base of the tallest tower, overseeing the work. Teams of laborers worked to erect wooden towers and scaffolds. Across the way, engineers were securing heavy rope lines into pulleys they had fastened to the valley wall. To Elinor, it looked as if a massive spider had begun to cocoon the keep in a dun-colored web of ropes and pulleys.

Con nodded as Elinor approached. "I've got everyone working double time," he said. "With everything that's happened, I thought we may want to get this done as quickly as possible."

Elinor frowned at that. "Everything that's happened?"

Con gave a few more commands to his aide, Petnar, then sent the small, bald man off. Con lowered his voice. "Tae spoke to me last night about what happened with her father and the Lady."

Frustration brought heat to her cheeks and Elinor gritted her teeth. "She did what? Of all the irresponsible—" she caught herself before her voice rose louder. "I told them to leave it. If someone had overheard, she could've gotten herself killed. Or you, for that matter."

Con held up a hand. "Give me some credit, Elinor. I made sure it was discreet."

"This is serious, Con. Whatever foolishness they have in their minds, they will bring the wrath of Piersym's entire entourage down upon everyone in this village."

"I'm well aware. I've looked at Ephed's eyes. That man is aching for any excuse to get his blade red."

"Exactly," Elinor said. "Then why the hell would she get you involved?"

Con puffed out his chest. "Haven't you heard? I'm rather famous. I've killed rendworms, you know." Her frown grew even deeper and Con's face lost its mirth. "Tae knows who you are," he said. "She pieced it together after your run in with Ephed. She was very young, but she was at Aegis while you were making waves at the Academy. She knows all the stories. It's why they went to you. Why they trusted you with their secret."

"And when she came to you, what did you tell her?"

"The truth," Con said. "That I have never known you to be wrong. That I trust you with my life to do what's right. And that, however hard, they too should trust in what you tell them."

Her shoulders slumping, Elinor blew out a breath that steamed in the morning chill. "To do what's right? You sound like you're still an academy cadet, Con," she said quietly.

"And what's wrong with that?"

Elinor was quiet for a moment, her eyes taking in the web of ropes that draped from the keep. "You've been in Resa all this time, Con. Out here, it's different. If Piersym and Ephed are responsible for the murder of Lady Lliane and her First Blade, then the damage has already been done. Even if Tae and Aebelm wanted to make their case before the warden, they would not live long enough to make their testimony. Timberline was doomed the moment Piersym decided he wanted it." She felt cold and hollow as she said the words.

Elinor felt a hand rest briefly on her shoulder. "It isn't any different in Resa either," Con said. "It's why I left. And I didn't come out to the marches because I thought it would be better. I came because I knew you would be." He squeezed her shoulder once and dropped his hand away. "I know it's never been a fair or easy road for you. I was there through the heart of it. But I can tell from the look in your eyes, you believe their story. These people need your help, Elinor."

In the two years since she had seen him, Elinor had forgotten how damned perceptive he could be. "They said Tae's father and Lady Lliane were married in the old way. Even if I could verify that, and even if I could somehow keep them alive long enough to make my claim to the warden, it would only put their necks under the blade, Con. They could never rest. Never hide. And even if they win this battle, then there'll be another and another until Tae, Aebelm, and everyone they care for end up as dead as Tae's father."

Con stared at her and Elinor felt the weight of his gaze like a stone around her neck. In his eyes, she saw the depth of his emotion. At first, she took it for disappointment, but then she realized what it truly was. Pity.

He gave a slow nod. "If you say we stay our hand, then we stay. I trust you." He lowered his brow, seeking her focus with his large brown eyes. "But Tae will not stand by and do nothing. You know that as well as I do. She has lost too much, and the men responsible for that loss are here within reach. She feels like she has nothing to lose, Elinor. What do you think she's going to do?"

This time, it was Elinor who was quiet.

"If you are sure there is nothing to be done, then you must talk to her again and be sure to stop whatever she has planned. You are the only one she'll listen to."

"Why?" Elinor asked. "Because she admires me?"

"No," Con said. "Because she is you. Or, the you I remember from that first day in the drowning grass. You are asking her to let this go. Ask yourself, Elinor. Could you?"

***

As Elinor came out onto the parapet, she saw Tae staring off into the distance, her slender silhouette standing out against the gray sky. A small storm lantern was at her side, a single candle burning inside the glass cage.

"You sit the Long Vigil for your father," Elinor said.

Tae turned. "You know of it?"

She felt old memories grip her heart. "I sat the Long Vigil for someone once. Her name was Lida," Elinor said quietly.

Tae's eyes widened. "I know the story, and what came after, of what you did. It's why I told my grandfather about you. It's why we believed in you." She had turned more fully toward Elinor, and she held the storm lantern against her chest as if she could protect the small flame burning inside even more than the lantern's glass.

Elinor met her gaze. "I know what you asked of me, but it cannot be. And if you will listen to me, I will explain to you why. Will you listen?"

Slowly, Tae nodded.

Elinor closed her eyes for a moment. "My first days at the Academy were hard. I entered with visions of glory and honor, fixated on the great deeds I would accomplish there. But the Academy I had sought to join was merely a storyteller's echo. The reality was the Academy had become the last refuge for the spoiled children of nobility, for those unable to become Razors and without the skills to succeed in the Collegium. They were dumped and forgotten there by their disappointed parents, and they used that as their excuse for cruelty.

"I tried to keep my head down and out of their way, but I was an orphan. I was a reminder that this was the best they could achieve, that even a nameless orphan could join them there.

"But then I met Lida. She believed in what the Academy had once been. She believed in what an officer could be. Was supposed to be. She was noble-born like most of the other cadets, but she offered me friendship." Elinor crossed her arms against a chill in the air. "Other cadets warned her not to, but she didn't back down. I was proud to call her my friend.

"But her actions drew attention from the worst of the cadets. I was an enemy to these people, but Lida? She was a traitor. Their hatred for her eclipsed even their feelings for me. There were threats to her, and her family got involved. Eventually, even I begged her to stay away." The burning in her throat and the stinging wetness of her eyes made it hard to speak, but Elinor continued on.

"One morning, she fell from a tower." Elinor said simply, her voice hollow. "It was said she jumped, but there was no investigation, no consequences. Even worse, word spread quickly who had truly been responsible. They wanted others to know they had done it, you see. To know what would happen to those who defied their power."

Tae nodded. "That's when you began to fight back. That's what made you go out and face the rendworms, and what drove you to defeat the Gauntlet. Even at Aegis, we heard about that. It was Lida's death that inspired you to such great acts."

"Yes," Elinor said, her heart like a leaden weight in her chest. "And when I graduated from the Academy and earned my commission, I learned exactly what all those great acts had achieved. What Lida's death had earned for me."

"What?" asked Tae, leaning closer.

"Nothing," Elinor said.

Tae sat back as if Elinor had physically struck her.

"I know how you feel, Tae. Believe me, I have been where you are," she said, her eyes looking down to the small flame in the lantern. "I've felt the anger, the rage at such callous injustice. But as time has gone on, I have learned a harsh lesson." The words slipped from her mouth, tasting like dust and old blood. "Lida died for nothing. She died for a dream, for something that isn't real. After everything I did in the Academy, it didn't make a damn difference. Nothing's changed. Behind an Ephed or Piersym is another Ephed or Piersym, and behind them, another and another."

Elinor sought the girl's eyes, boring into her with icy blue intensity. "This is not a battle that can be won, Tae. Pursuing it will only bring misery or death. And not only to you, but to those you care for and love. I know it's hard, but you just have to accept it and move on."

Tae did not respond. The only sound the wind rushing through the valley. Finally, with tears standing in her eyes, Tae shook her head. "I can't. I can't just accept this."

"I am sorry, Tae."

"You don't understand, Elinor. But you will, if you will just come with me to the Stone Altar. It is where my father and the Lady Lliane were killed. Come there and see, and then you will understand."

"Tae—"

The girl gripped Elinor's hand, holding it tightly. "Please, Elinor. Just come and see. I promise you, it will change everything."

Before Elinor could answer, the sound of boots on stone caused her to turn around.

Ephed walked toward them.

"Lord Piersym demands your presence, Reaper," he said, accentuating the title.

Elinor feared they had been overheard, but she put a smile on her face. "Find your grandfather, Tae. We'll have a chance to share more stories later," she said. She smiled broadly, but her eyes warned Tae to leave. The girl bowed and backed away.

Ephed turned back toward the keep.

Gritting her teeth, Elinor fell into step beside him.

ACT 4

"You spend a great deal of time with the common folk," Ephed said as they walked. His tone was light, but he carried himself taut, like a coiled serpent ready to strike. "No doubt a product of your upbringing, eh orphan? Like seeks like, I find."

"Then I suppose I should be grateful that you were able to pry yourself away from the brothels long enough to act as my escort," she shot back in an easy tone.

From the corner of her eye, she saw the muscles in his face twitch with anger. Good, she thought. The more his attention was focused on her, the blinder he would be to Tae.

Ephed's voice lowered. "We've had our fun, Reaper. But I would not push things if I were you."

"And I would not start things I could not finish, if I were you, Razor. I am here to do my duty and nothing further."

"We shall see," Ephed said.

His answer surprised her, and she wondered how long he had been at that doorway before he let his presence be known. Was he insinuating something?

They had made their way through the length of the keep and climbed the primary tower. Ephed opened the door to the master chamber. It had once belonged to Lady Lliane, but Piersym had wasted no time appropriating it as his own.

Lord Piersym sat on a large chair, fine blankets draped around it. In his hand, he gripped an ornate bottle of wine and as Elinor entered the room, she heard the rhythmic tapping of one of his large rings against the glass.

He turned his heavy-joweled face to regard her with small, piggish eyes. "Come, come," he said, gesturing wildly. For Elinor, it seemed there was a sense of impatience in every word, every movement the man made.

"Lord Piersym," Elinor said, coming to attention and offering a salute.

Piersym ignored it completely. "Is everything in order for the ceremony, Reaper?"

"Yes," Elinor said, choking back her distaste for him. "The ceremony should be able to take place tomorrow. We are making arrangements with the household staff to accommodate the size of your retinue but things—"

"Yes, yes. There is no time to waste. Every minute here is a lifetime I am away from Resa. Things move quickly there, Reaper, and I am missing them. I need things to move quickly here as well. No problems and no delays."

"I understand," Elinor said simply, her voice cool and direct.

Piersym halted his tapping. "I am aware of your past conflicts, you know. To tell the truth, I was warned that I should refuse to use you. That I should demand another officer to act as Reaper for this process. Do you know why I decided to keep you?" he asked, leaning forward with a growing smile.

"No," Elinor answered.

"You were the cheapest," Piersym said and laughed loudly, seemingly tickled with his own wit. "Other Reapers cost, you see. They bleed you here and there with bribes to expedite things. But you? Why, you do your duty, Lieutenant. And duty doesn't cost me a single coin."

Elinor knew what Piersym spoke of was common practice, but to have him speak of it so blatantly, so openly, was both insulting and shameful. Elinor gritted her teeth, but remained silent.

Piersym took a long pull of the bottle, smacking his lips after and staring longingly at the shaped glass. "How long has it been since you've been to Resa, Lieutenant?"

"Two years," she said.

Piersym made a strangled cough. "Two years?" he exclaimed. "That's an eternity. Practically a death sentence, isn't it, Ephed?"

"Indeed, my lord. Easier to be dead," Ephed said, and she could hear him savoring every word.

Piersym shook his head. "Resa is everything, Lieutentant. It is the future. It is life itself. The marches," he said, gesturing dismissively with the bottle, red wine spilling onto the floor, "are nothing but farms and lumber and bandits and savagery. The purpose of the marches is to feed Resa, like blood to the heart."

Elinor's eyes focused on the small pool of red wine staining the pale stone.

"I must settle my affairs here in Timberline quickly and cleanly," he said. "Play your part in this little charade of ceremony well, Reaper, and I can get you back to Resa. Perhaps I will even champion your career. I have destroyed enough officer's careers. It might be a bit of an enjoyable diversion to try and rebuild one instead."

Elinor nodded and offered a tight smile, but something stuck in her mind. The way he spoke of settling his affairs here, the way that Ephed had smiled at those words. She knew she should stay quiet. That if she did, this meeting would be over soon. And yet...

"Securing Timberline was indeed fortunate for you, Lord Piersym," she said.

Piersym's eyes narrowed. "Fortune had nothing to do with it. Fortune is for the weak, for those who gamble their lives away in Resa's Razor pits." He leaned forward, pointing with his finger for emphasis. "Power is the true game. The only game. Power is what brought me Timberline."

In that moment, she saw it. The look in his eyes and Ephed's as well. Neither bothered to hide it. The smug satisfaction.

These men had killed Lady Lliane and her First Blade.

And they wanted Elinor to know it.

Piersym wanted her to know what he had done, and to know there was nothing anyone could do about it. He gloried in it.

Elinor had seen eyes like that before. Perhaps because the memory was so fresh in her mind after sharing it with Tae, but it filled her thoughts now. That look of control, of power. Of cruelty and mockery. Of sublime arrogance. It was the same expression the cadets at the Academy had used to break those they deemed lesser. It was the expression she had seen when they told her what had happened with Lida.

The rage kindled inside her, a burning coal in the pit of her stomach. Piersym spoke, and she nodded, but all she wanted to do was flee the room before she could no longer hold it in.

At last, Piersym dismissed her with a final wave of his hand. Elinor turned smartly and strode from the room, not bothering to look at Ephed as she passed. Once she was clear of the door, she took the stairs two at a time.

Her thoughts were swirling, and her long legs ate up the steps in long strides. She made a direct line to the village.

Outside of a small house, Aebelm and Tae were talking together quietly. They both looked up as Elinor approached.

"Take me to where they were killed," Elinor said. "Take me to the Stone Altar."

They traveled out of the ravine and up onto the forested plateau. The path through the thick forest was narrow, and they rode for the better part of an hour.

In the heart of the forest, amidst the rustling trees, Elinor felt something powerful and heavy, as if the very air itself carried a sense of sorrow and mourning. She immediately chastised herself. It was the melancholy of her companions affecting her. The depth of their tragedy speaking to her and her own heart responding. And yet, the closer they got to the Stone Altar, the stronger it seemed to grow.

Ahead, the forest opened into a clearing. Light played over vibrant green foliage, and Elinor gazed around at the spectacular beauty. They were on the very edge of the plateau, and the rest of the march stretched green and vibrant all the way to the horizon. It was like standing on the top of the world.

Old stonework, ancient beyond her ability to figure, delineated the clearing. Now, after centuries, the forest had reclaimed what had been the home of men and enveloped it in verdant life. The central piece of the old construction was a wide set of stone steps that led up to a small, ruined altar.

"It is truly beautiful here. Sacred," Elinor said. "I understand your feelings about this place now." As she spoke, both grandfather and granddaughter were staring at the broken altar.

"Something is not right," Aebelm said. "We brought you here to see," he said, emphasizing the last word, and there was frustration and disappointment in his voice.

As Aebelm began to shake his head, something shifted in the air and Elinor felt the skin on the back of her neck pricking.

From the far side of the clearing, a voice came smooth and supremely arrogant. "The most surprising thing about killing a noble," Ephed said, stepping into view. "Is that it is so much easier than you would imagine. Turns out that the blood of nobles spills just as easily as any other."

Elinor went cold as more men emerged from the forest. Razors. Ten in all. Two Razors would have been a difficult proposition to handle. This many, though? There was no hope.

A voice in her head screamed, railing at her stupidity and carelessness. She pushed it aside and drew herself up tall to face Ephed. "The lady of this land is murdered. Your lord is responsible. You were merely following his orders, I am sure. The Warden may still grant leniency if you cooperate," she said, her voice projecting authority.

Ephed raised his eyebrows. "That's it? That's your play, Reaper? Truly you disappoint me." He took a single step forward and, despite the distance between them, Elinor felt trapped. "You know, Piersym feared you would interfere. But me? I hoped you would," he said with a predator's smile. "I prayed for it."

"Then let me answer your prayers, Razor. You've done enough to Timberline. Let the others go and then you and I can at last have that fight you've been itching for. Let's finally see which of us is better." She rested one hand on the sheathed blade at her belt and the other brought her mace up to her shoulder.

The other Razors stepped forward, but Ephed held up a hand with a laugh.

Then, she felt it. A surge of electricity in the air. The telltale sign of a Razor drawing upon the essence of the world to fuel their power.

Elinor felt it like a wave of pressure rolling off Ephed and enveloping her, almost as if she was underwater. The energy existed in the air between them, slowing time itself.

Ephed moved faster than she could have imagined.

He was upon her, his attacks moving at blinding speed. She brought the mace across her body, shielding her vital organs. She could not match his speed, so she weathered the storm, protecting her core as he sliced lines of fire into her arms and sides.

As his assault began to slow, Elinor readied herself to strike back. Then the wave of energy came once more and his foot lashed out, taking her in the chest. She tumbled backwards, rolling to the edge of the cliff.

Ephed held his blade, the bright steel stained red with her blood. "Well, I believe we have our answer," he said with a smile. "You lose, Reaper."

Aebelm moved in front of Elinor's downed form as Tae rushed to her side.

Elinor got to her knees. "Run," she hissed at the girl and the old man. "You must survive this or their secret dies here with us!"

Ephed snapped his blade, and drops of Elinor's blood hit the stone beneath him. The clearing filled with electricity as the Razors touched their power and moved forward.

Waves of energy rolled off Aebelm as the old Razor drew his sword and readied his shield. Tae stood tall beside him.

"Run!" Elinor yelled.

And then there was chaos and blood.

The first Razors came forward and Aebelm charged to meet them. Blood flew through the air and the sound of steel upon steel shattered the quiet.

Another Razor came for Tae. As the girl raised her blade, the Razor lashed out, taking her blade high and wide before thrusting his sword into Tae's stomach. The girl's eyes widened. Her sword dropped from her hand, and she toppled toward the cliff's edge.

Elinor rushed forward and slid, avoiding the Razor's attack. Her mace cracked into his knee and he cried out. As he fell backward, she dropped her mace and grabbed hold of Tae.

A shadow loomed over Elinor and hot blood sprayed on her back. Aebelm stood there, blood covering his face. He had intercepted the blow intended for her. Waves of power radiated from him, washing over her.

Aebelm locked eyes with her, blue irises glittering like diamonds in the dark mask of blood. "Go," he whispered.

Behind him, Ephed raised his blade once more, and the light in Aebelm's eyes was taken from the world forever.

Gripping Tae tightly, Elinor rolled off the edge toward a small ledge. She barely managed to catch it, but Tae missed. Elinor's arm wrenched from the full weight of the falling girl, and she screamed, scrambling for purchase with her free arm as the girl's weight pulled her down.

Elinor's body dangled off the side, one hand desperately holding the ledge, Tae swinging limply from the other. Her shoulder burned with pain, and she did not have the strength to pull the girl up.

"Let... let me... go," Tae whispered, her eyes barely open.

"I won't let you fall," Elinor said through gritted teeth, but the slide of dirt under her hand threatened to prove that a lie.

At the top of the cliff, Ephed and his Razors looked down upon her struggles. As her fingers continued to slip, Ephed smiled.

Then, the dirt beneath her hand gave way, and Elinor and Tae plummeted down.

ACT 5

From the depths of darkness, Elinor clawed her way back to consciousness. She took a deep breath and pain flared in her chest, bright and sharp, forcing her eyes wide and causing her to release a strangled gasp.

Her left arm hung limp. She tried pushing herself up, but that motion brought more agony and she bit down hard to keep from screaming. No screams lest her enemies find her.

Elinor had no illusions that surviving the fall meant real safety. A man like Ephed would not assume she was dead until he had her head in his hands. Already, his Razors would be looking to confirm their deaths.

Near her outstretched arm, Tae lay unconscious, breathing softly, the grass beneath her stained red. Everywhere around them, tall, green grass obscured her vision.

Elinor tried to rise. Each breath was a stab of raw agony, and she feared a broken rib might have punctured a lung. She lay back and forced herself to slow her breathing.

Amidst her suffering, one thought echoed relentlessly in her mind.

She had failed.

She had failed Tae. Failed Aebelm. Failed herself.

She had been naive. The old ways were as dead as the old man Aebelm. As dead as his son and the Lady of Timberline. As dead as his granddaughter, Tae, would soon be.

They had put their faith in her, and she had failed them.

"No," she whispered. There was such fierce anger behind the word that it even surprised her. Her eyes stung with tears.

Tears of rage.

"No," she said again, and this time she forced a deep breath. Her good hand clenched, gripping at the ground. The feel of cool earth on her skin felt good.

It reminded her that she still lived.

And if she still lived, then she could still fight. Today was no different than any other day. The choice was there. Fight or run. Rise or die.

Elinor's hand dug into the mud, and slowly, inch by inch, Elinor pulled herself up. Ignoring the pain, ignoring the weakness, she drew herself up until at last she stood tall, looking over the expanse of waving grass.

She steadied herself. Then, opening her eyes, she realized why the bright green stalks of grass seemed so familiar.

It was drowning grass.

An ocean of drowning grass.

Elinor froze, keeping her body as still as possible, willing her wobbling legs to steady themselves. She heard distant voices. They were faint, coming from around the plateau, but distinct nonetheless. Elinor knew their source: Ephed's Razors.

As quickly as she dared, Elinor moved to Tae. The girl was pale, her skin a chalky white. Blood seeped from her abdomen, and Tae's chest rose and fell with faint, shallow breaths. Elinor tore strips from her leggings and bound the wound as best she could.

She tried getting Tae onto her back, but it was no use. With only one working arm, she could not lift Tae's limp body.

The voices of the Razors sounded again, and Elinor saw flaming torches in the fading gray of evening. There was no attempt at subterfuge. She knew the Razors sought to flush them out and rattle them into making a run for it, so they could bring them down like hunting dogs on their prey.

Elinor eased some of the long blades of grass over Tae, hiding her, and set off carefully. A lone tree loomed ahead, its limbs twisting toward the sun. Clearing the distance to it, she climbed atop the giant roots at its base.

Behind her, Elinor heard cruel laughter, and she could see them now.

Razors. Four of them, moving into the grass.

Elinor bared her teeth in an expression of savage rage. She braced her good arm around the tree and slammed her shoulder against the hard wood with a scream of pain and defiance.

There was a sickening pop as her shoulder slipped back into place, and her vision grayed to a dark tunnel.

The Razors rushed toward her.

Reaching down, Elinor drew her officer's sword. She walked into the grass and raised her blade high.

Still, she told herself. No matter what. Stay still. Stay silent.

The Razors were close enough that Elinor saw the color of their eyes.

Then the earth before her erupted.

A massive form burst from the ground, writhing and screaming like a mountain being birthed. Flying grass and a cascade of dirt blurred her vision, but through this cloud, she caught sight of something that pushed her to the brink of madness.

A giant pillar of flesh, rising higher than the keep's tower.

Elinor gaped at the impossibility before her. Every fiber of her screamed to run, to flee, but she held her ground, holding her breath in hope she might remain beneath its notice.

Turning in on itself, the creature twisted back down, the front of it opening like a nightmare flower. Within the open maw, writhing tentacles snapped and whipped.

The Razors were scattered by the force of the colossus's arrival. One man dropped to his knees and screamed incoherently. The others ran.

The first man was taken almost faster than Elinor could track, disappearing in a fountain of dirt and a maelstrom of rippling grass. A massive tentacle reared up, coiling around him and flailing him like a petulant child with a broken toy.

The rendworms she had faced long ago had been terrible creatures, but their barbed tentacles had been about as wide as a rope. The tentacle that gripped the man was the size of a wagon. It swung him high in the air, his screams a horrifying mix of terror and madness.

A Tyrant.

Not the feared rendworms that descended from them, but an actual Earth Tyrant, the likes of which great Aedan and brave Garhard had bested in the old story.

Elinor watched as a creature of legend fed, tossing her screaming enemies into its maw. The Tyrant devoured the last Razor and then began sliding across the grass in Elinor's direction.

Elinor held still, forcing even her thoughts quiet. Iron discipline warred with the primal urge to flee, but Elinor kept her place.

Stay still. Stay silent.

The Tyrant slid past her, close enough that its smell, like rich soil and old growth, filled her nostrils. The wake of its passage rolled under her like ocean waves. Then, smoothly and with an undulating grace that belied its enormous size, the Tyrant slid back into the earth. The drowning grass was impossibly pristine, as if Elinor had imagined the entire event.

Of the four Razors who had come to kill her, there was no sign.

Slowly, she raised a hand to wipe away the layer of dirt covering her face. Unbidden, the words of the ancient story came to her lips. "And from the sea of Earth, where the Tyrants ruled, did Aedan and Garhard pass, seeking the Shepherd of Tree and Stone."

Her mind flashed back to the massive tapestry hanging in the keep. The view depicted there was the same she had stared out upon at the top of the plateau. Suddenly, all of Aebelm's subtle words and prodding came screaming to the fore of her mind. This was what he had been trying to tell her. Timberline was sacred because it was where myth had one day been truth.

This was the land of the story.

Overcome by this revelation, long moments of silence passed before Elinor moved back to Tae. Though the Razors were gone, she knew Tae would not last much longer. A return to the village was impossible, and crossing the domain of the Tyrant with the girl seemed just as unlikely. There was nowhere to go. No way to save her.

The part of Elinor that had risen from the grass in defiance of death snarled at impossibility. It seized upon the memory of the story, rolling the words around over and over until they slipped from Elinor's bloodstained lips like a prayer.

The Shepherd of Tree and Stone.

In the story, Aedan had called out to the ancient spirit and it had answered. Elinor felt the blood seeping from her own wounds. It stained her hand red as she clenched it into a fist. Her thoughts coalesced into a crystal-clear idea. It was a foolish idea, an impossible hope from a girl who had read too many stories as a child.

Elinor smiled grimly.

She stood in the Vale of Tyrants, where Aedan himself had walked. This was no time to be cowed by what was deemed possible.

She raised her bloody fist before her. "To the Shepherd of Tree and Stone. I call to you. I stand with blood and earth and call to you."

With force, she drove her bloody fist into the soft earth, feeling the soil mingle with her blood. Then, she felt it. A thrum, deep and low in the earth.

Once.

Then again.

It came slowly, but more and more steadily. It throbbed across the immense expanse of the drowning grass, causing the tall blades to twitch and shake.

It felt like a heartbeat.

The force of it was powerful. Greater than the Tyrant, greater than storm or sun or wind. It was the slow pounding of stone against stone, coming from the tall cliff of the plateau. As her eyes traced up, boulders shook and tumbled down.

One landed heavily in the drowning grass. Elinor steeled herself for the return of the Tyrant, but there was nothing. Nothing save the beating heart of the world she now felt in her own blood.

A sound that was half-laugh, half-gasp escaped her lips. She felt lightheaded, but whether from injuries or madness, she did not know.

The sheer height of the climb seemed impossible and she would have to carry Tae through the drowning grass even before that. And yet there was no decision to be made.

"I come," Elinor whispered, her voice thick with exhaustion and amazement.

Elinor picked up Tae's unconscious form, settling the girl on her back. Closing her eyes, she stepped onto the drowning grass.

She moved steadily, with no stealth or art, one foot after the other into the realm of the Tyrant, but the drowning grass remained calm as she passed. And, as if it knew she answered the invitation of something older than myth, the Tyrant did not return.

Elinor circled the plateau's wide base and spied a break in the scrub where a path opened. She began the ascent, moving with all the speed she could manage, but the ground was rough and uneven. As she pushed on, her ankle twisted sharply, and she stumbled, screaming in pain from her broken ribs. She stopped to catch her breath but kept climbing.

The sun died as the moon and stars rose high in the night sky. In the pale light, the path was difficult to follow and Elinor's pace slowed. Tae's breathing grew shallower as they climbed. Warm blood seeped onto Elinor's back.

Yet, she pushed on, driven by a faith that transcended rational thought.

Finally, through the trees she caught sight of the ruins. The old man's body was where she remembered, stretched out by the far edge of the cliff. Even in death, his face was resolute. Elinor bowed her head in deference before moving on.

The stone structure of the ruins was different. A wide, round chasm was now open at the base of the stairs.

Legs shaking with exhaustion, Elinor carried Tae down into the earth. She trudged on, until at last the cavern opened into a massive space. Milky white crystals in the walls bathed everything in a soft light.

As she stepped from the final stair, Elinor collapsed to her knees. Light from crystals illuminated veins of silver, crossing through the rock like a spiderweb of moonlight.

Slowly, a stone began to move across the floor. Another followed it, and then even more. Stones, gems, and the roots of trees flowed and moved in a swirling eddy, like the waves of a great ocean.

There were no words, even if Elinor had the strength to form them. Tears flowed down her face as she stared. Where the Tyrant's arrival had brought horror and madness, this time there was only awe as stone and earth shaped itself into being. It moved with an almost musical sound, as each piece flowed together, forming a creature of impossible grace and motion.

Finally, the tide of earth and stone receded, drawing up like an immense cresting wave. It towered over Elinor and Tae, threatening to engulf the two in a massive cascade of rock. From within the stone wave, two large crystals flowed to the surface, glowing with milky white light.

The Shepherd of Tree and Stone stared down at them.

Elinor felt the weight of those eyes, like all the mountains of the world pressed down upon her. Slowly, she moved Tae's limp form forward.

The rolling tide of root and stone flowed, bringing bright, glowing eyes closer to Tae. Then, it was still, and silence filled the room.

"I have brought her here," Elinor said. "Please. Save her."

The Shepherd of Tree and Stone swayed back and forth, but it did not move to help her.

"I don't... I don't understand. Are you the Shepherd of Tree and Stone?"

The response came as much in her heart and mind as in her ears. "That is what your kind has often called me," the Shepherd intoned. The powerful response resonated in her very bones.

"She is a daughter of Timberline. Her people have honored you since the days of Aedan. Please, you must save her."

The immense wall of stone flowed like water once more. Now it resembled a long, arcing neck, its glowing crystal eyes focusing intense light. That feeling in heart and mind came again to Elinor as the spirit spoke, "I can only do what I can do. Nothing more."

There was a sadness from the otherworldly creature with those words, and Elinor felt it take hold. A sadness and a certainty.

The Shepherd could not save Tae.

"Why?" she whispered, her eyes filling with tears. "Why did you show me the way here if not to save her?" She shook her head in disbelief. "Why bring me here?"

Images came. Elinor looked down upon herself from a great height, standing in a sea of waving green. She saw herself raise her fist and call out, her voice clear.

"You brought yourself here," the Shepherd said, the ancient voice filling her.

Elinor sank down as the true weight of loss filled her. "I came here to save her," she whispered.

In her mind, images coalesced. A swath of forest burned to twisted, black ruins. A delicate natural arch of stone giving way under one final flake of snow. The last leaves clinging to a branch as bitter winds swirled around it.

"Some things cannot be saved," spoke the Shepherd.

There was a feeling of deep sadness, and it was more than she could bear. Elinor knelt in the shadow of the ancient spirit and wept. Her sobs stole the air from her lungs, and for a brief moment, she could not breathe or speak. Then, she drew in a deep ragged breath and savagely wiped a hand across her eyes.

"No," Elinor said. "I cannot accept this."

A feather-light touch caught her attention and she looked down in surprise. Tae was reaching for her hand, small fingers trembling. Elinor grabbed her hand and Tae slowly smiled, her teeth stained with blood.

"It's all right. I chose this. And now you know," Tae said, her eyes on the towering shape of the Shepherd. "Now you have seen. I've done my part and that's enough for me." With that, her eyes began to close.

Elinor felt the flutter of life in her hand fading and she squeezed it between both of her own. "Don't you give up, Tae. Tae!"

Grief and rage erupted from Elinor. "Do something, damn you! I know you can. I know it."

The Shepherd did not move, but continued regarding her with unblinking eyes.

"You helped Aedan in the darkest times," Elinor said, driven by her memories of the stories that had sustained her through her own darkest days. "You performed magic and miracles well beyond what I am asking of you." She gestured down to Tae. "How can you turn your back now? This girl, her entire family, have given everything to protect you. To serve you!"

"And what have you given?"

The question echoed in her chest, in her mind, and she felt its vibration in her bones and teeth. It stunned her into silence. The Shepherd's form grew larger, flowing closer to her, until those glowing, crystal eyes were directly in front of her. She became lost in the light of them, the eternity of them.

"There is a balance to all things," the Shepherd intoned. In her mind, a pristine beach stretched endlessly to the horizon. Then the vision focused down to a single grain of sand. It moved slightly in a breeze, and as it did, the grains next to it shifted, and then more and more moved across the sandy dunes. "What you call magic or miracles is simply the movement of that balance." And then, just like that, the sand was gone and Elinor was back staring into ancient eyes. "There is always a cost."

Elinor's mind was reeling, but in the palm of her hand, she felt Tae's faint pulse. "Whatever it is. I will pay it."

"Like him, you are quick to answer."

She fought to understand the spirit's words. Was it referring to Aedan? That thought only served to embolden her. "Not quick," she replied, her voice growing stronger. "Prepared. Tell me what I must do, Old One, and it shall be done."

Its eyes remained still and unblinking. "That is not for me to decide, Child of Aedan."

Her mind reached back through the stories and legends she knew so well, and she found the answer: an offering of devotion. A show of worth. That is what had won great Aedan the Shepherd's favor.

She raised her chin. "I shall finish the fight that has cost Tae and her family so much. I shall give her justice." She opened her mouth and spoke words that she had once believed only existed in ancient stories, "By blood and water. By breath and wind. By bone and stone. Thrice said, thrice bound. I offer my oath."

The stone softened and flowed, wrapping the girl's body as gently as a blanket. In Elinor's mind, she saw images. In the center of the old ruins, stood a man and a woman. The man wore the colors of Timberline and the woman an old-fashioned dress. They held hands and stared into each other's eyes. It was the wedding of Lady Lliane and Tae's father.

The images faded slowly and, as she regained her sight, Elinor saw Tae's face relax in a gentle smile. Her breathing grew quiet and easy.

Elinor let out a deep breath. "You opened a way for me here. Now, I ask for a way out so that I may fulfill my oath."

The stone wave shifted, and Tae was gently moved along like a flower petal on the surface of a lake. Across the cavern, there was a hiss of shifting earth. A length of dark tunnel emerged, and at its end, an opening that looked upon a village.

Last Dawn Keep loomed behind it.

"Rest easy, Tae," she whispered to the air. "This is my fight now."

Elinor placed her hand on her heart in the old manner, then turned and strode down the tunnel to fulfill her promise.

Act 6

The air was crisp and cold as Elinor stepped out into the dim light of evening. She had stepped from the stone wall of a watchtower, but there was no hole now, only smooth gray lines separating the wall's stones.

Elinor approached the village, careful to stay out of the brighter pockets of moonlight. Her shoulder ached and various cuts oozed dark blood. The worst were her broken ribs, still sending stabbing pains every time she took a deep breath.

The streets were quiet and empty as Elinor located Bilia's house. Her vision was blurry and she swayed unsteadily, but she finally found it. She slumped against the door, knocking weakly.

Elinor slipped forward as the door opened, but Bilia caught her. "What is it, girl? What's happened?" she asked, struggling to carry Elinor inside.

"Piersym's men attacked us. Aebelm... Tae... I'm sorry, Bilia," Elinor said, her eyes filled with tears.

Bilia recoiled like she had been slapped. A strangled gasp escaped her lips before she wrapped Elinor in a tight embrace. "You are hurt," the old woman managed to say. "Let's get you inside."

Bilia set Elinor down on a chair. The old woman stood up, wiped a tear from her cheek, and lit a candle off embers in the fireplace.

"What do you need?" Bilia asked, her voice low and even, a calm veneer over the sorrow in her eyes.

"Con," Elinor said, gritting through the pain. "I need Conbert here now. And he needs to bring a map of the keep." She paused to take a few shallow breaths. "And then I will need you to get word to all in the village who you can trust." She looked Bilia in the eyes. "I failed to save your family, Bilia. I will not fail to see them get justice."

Bilia nodded before moving to a low shelf by the door. She returned with a needle and fine thread. "Best to get started putting yourself back together then while I go fetch your engineer." The old woman grabbed a shawl by the door and headed out into the night.

Elinor stitched. The work was slow and her injured left arm was clumsy, but she managed to close up the worst cuts before Bilia returned.

Con entered, his eyes wide. "Aedan's blood, Elinor!" he gasped, kneeling beside her.

"Ephed. Is he back yet?" Elinor asked.

"I never saw him leave, but he returned with only six of his Razors around sunset. He said you were off dealing with some local matters with Tae and Aebelm." He frowned, his brow furrowing. "What do you need from me, Elinor?"

"The ceremony. Has it happened yet?"

"Not yet. But Lord Piersym has been raising a fuss, complaining about you going off and demanding that I go through with it as King's Representative in your place. I've been stalling him, though."

"Good," Elinor said, closing her eyes. "Then that is where we will take them. When they're all together and their minds are focused on their victory."

"Elinor. We cannot take on that many Razors. Not even with the whole village armed and at our backs. It would be a massacre."

"No. It won't come to that," Elinor said. "Did you bring the map?"

Con reached into his satchel and produced a piece of vellum.

Elinor leaned over it. "Where is the most secure point in the keep?" she asked. "If Piersym were threatened, where would he seek refuge?"

"The tallest tower," Con said, and Bilia nodded.

"Good," she exhaled.

"What in the hells are you planning, Elinor?" Con asked. "What do you think we have that can stand against so many?"

Elinor closed her eyes and sat back in the chair. "The only thing that's stronger than a Razor's steel," she said. A slight smile tugged at the corner of her mouth when there was no reply.

"Stone."

***

Bright sunlight shone through the tall windows of the main hall, and loud voices echoed off the high walls. Leaning against the stone alcove, Elinor kept the hood of the robe up over her head and remained out of sight.

The various militia soldiers and hangers-on who had accompanied Piersym to Timberline were in place for the Ceremony of Reclamation that would see him officially installed as the new Lord of Timberline.

Piersym entered, dressed in flowing robes more suitable to a king than the lord of two outlying marches. Ephed walked behind him, wearing the dark maroon of Hearthfire.

To Elinor's eyes, he looked drenched in old blood.

From outside, there was heavy sound like metal on rock, then a brief grinding. Some of the assembled looked confused, but when the noise faded, they appeared to return their attention to the air of impatience in the room.

After more clangs, Piersym yelled out, "Ephed, go see what that engineer is playing about with out there and get this farce started!"

As Ephed stood to leave, Elinor stepped out of the alcove, the heavy cloak of the king's black concealing her. She moved to the front of the hall and all attention shifted to her.

Piersym adjusted his heavy robes. "I am not accustomed to being made to wait, Engineer. You would do wise to remember that," the lord said with menace. "I am a man of great influence."

"What you are," Elinor said, pulling back the hood to reveal her face, "is an accomplice to murder and a traitor to the crown." She threw the cloak aside as her voice rang out in the hall. "Piersym of Hearthfire and Ephed, First Blade, I name you murderers. I name you oathbreakers. You have violated the Covenant of the First Ascended and broken faith with your king. And you shall answer for these crimes." She gestured to the others in the room. "All of you assembled here. You have one chance to exonerate yourself from complicity in the crimes of these traitors. Leave now or be judged alongside them."

From across the hall, Ephed glared at her. "You should have had sense enough to die out there, Reaper," he said slowly while drawing his blade.

Elinor met his gaze and smiled fiercely. "Had you truly been as good as you think you are, Razor, I would have."

Piersym's face turned a mottled purple. "Kill her!" he screamed.

The hall sprang into life as Razors drew their weapons and surged forward. The crowd erupted into chaos.

Elinor darted through the alcove and ran up a wide set of stairs. Her ribs screamed in protest as her breath came harsh and ragged. Still, she pushed on, taking steps two at a time. The clang and grind came again, closer now, almost matching the rhythm of her stride.

Behind her, Razors drew closer.

Elinor arrived at a broad stone landing, high up in the keep's secondary tower. She threw open the door and ran out onto the rampart, sprinting toward the edge.

Tied off there was a thick length of rope that led away from the keep to one of Con's tall wooden towers. As the first of the pursuing Razors emerged onto the parapet, Elinor grabbed the rope and leaped into the open air. She bit back a scream as her injured body swung across the open space between the two towers.

As she did, there was a final sound like a metal drum being struck and then a sharp series of cracks. A cacophony erupted as the tower she had leaped from tumbled down. Mixed with the roar of falling stone and the twang of pulling ropes, Elinor heard the shocked screams of the Razors as the tower collapsed under them.

Con's pulleys and ropes were arrayed around the remaining tower like a web, and his work crews ran furiously to and from their stations as they operated the heavy machinery.

Elinor swung the rest of the way to the far tower, reaching out her good arm and grabbing hold of an open window. The sudden arresting of her motion jarred her body and she felt stitches tear free. Warm blood cascaded down, but she pulled herself inside.

Her ears rang with the echo of the tower's destruction and her body felt strained and worn, but she forced herself to her feet and secured the rope beside the window. The real fight had not begun, and she would not let herself rest yet. She looked around and exhaled, trying to get what breath she could.

The door at the opposite end of the room flew open and Lord Piersym entered. His robes were disheveled, and his face still flushed. "You!" he shouted. "How dare you? Do you know who I am? My blood is the blood of the First Ascended. My lineage extends back to the time of legends! You dare to threaten me?"

Ephed emerged through the door, his blade in hand. "And just when I thought you would cheat me of my pleasure, Reaper, you come here to offer the gift of your death. I am touched you would be so gracious."

Elinor only half-listened to his threats. More clanking could be heard as the winches around the keep continued their work.

Elinor's eyes focused on Ephed and she drew her blade, moving into a position of guard. She slashed at him, but he sidestepped, moving closer to her. There was a blur, and she felt a cut open across her side, inches under the cut he had given her at the ruins.

Elinor swung at him again, and this time he met her blade with his own. She snarled as she stabbed at his eyes with her free hand. It forced him back and gave her a brief opening. Her blade scored along his side, drawing blood.

She felt electric flare, bright and hot, as Ephed's power burned and his speed increased.

What had started as attack shifted into a desperate defense as Elinor fought to keep his blade away. She stepped back, trying to gain space, but Ephed did not press. Instead, he too took a step back.

It was then Elinor noticed he had maneuvered her around so he was by the open window.

Ephed grabbed hold of the rope Elinor had left. "Did you truly think me so stupid, Reaper?" The sounds of the winches and pulleys came faster and the tower shook. Behind her, Elinor heard Piersym whimper.

Ephed smiled. "I could have killed you many times, but the truth is, Reaper, you simply aren't worth the effort."

Elinor launched an attack at Ephed, and he raised his blade to turn it aside. As he did, Elinor grabbed his weapon, the keen edge cutting into the flesh of her hand. Blood flowed down her arm as she swung her own blade toward Ephed's head. It whistled past as he ducked out of the way. He took her legs out with a swift kick, dropping her to the floor. Her broken ribs flared, and she screamed out.

Despite the pain, Elinor looked up in defiance and smiled. "You… lose," she gasped.

Ephed stared at the length of rope hanging limp in his hand. The rope she had just cut. Beyond the open window, the rest of it glided away, out of reach.

The room shook and groaned.

"You fool," Ephed spat. "Now we will both die. We all lose!"

Elinor drew herself up tall. "No, murderer, I came here to avenge the death of the Lady Lliane of Timberline and the family of Blades that served her. The men and women you slaughtered." The floor began to tremble and crack. "And now I have."

The tower shook and swayed. Then the room split, stone shattering and shrieking as the tower collapsed.

The world pitched and spun as the room crumbled, and they both fell.

She should have said goodbye to Conbert, she thought, as the world collapsed into chaos.

And then, just as she was closing her eyes, she felt a hand grip her arm. She looked, expecting to see Ephed's snarling face, but instead a thin arm was reaching through a circular hole in the stone wall.

The arm pulled hard, and Elinor slipped into the darkness of the hole.

She found herself once again in the cavern of the Shepherd of Tree and Stone. The roaring destruction of the collapsing keep was gone, replaced with a serene silence. Holding onto her arm, pale and gasping, was Tae.

The girl smiled at Elinor's confusion. "I will… not… let you fall," Tae said, and then closed her eyes.

EPILOGUE

Elinor and Con watched from a distance as the flames from Aebelm's funeral pyre flared into life. Elinor's left arm was wrapped in a makeshift sling, and tears filled her eyes as smoke rose into the sky.

Last Dawn Keep was a tumbled ruin. The two towers were shattered, and anything they had hit had been crushed as well. The outermost walls of the main keep remained whole, however, and it gave the impression of a wounded animal of cold, gray rock.

A long line of people stretched through the town, almost to the mouth of the ravine. Elinor was sure that the entire population of Timberline March had come.

The large gate to Last Dawn Keep remained standing, a lone arch of perfect stonework amidst the ruins. In the shadow of that arch, Tae and Bilia stood, receiving all who had come to pay their respects to the fallen Aebelm.

Tae's injuries had been severe, but she insisted she was strong enough to stand in the place of honor and say farewell to her grandfather properly. The girl was pale and leaned on a cane, but despite this, she stood tall as she greeted each person.

Elinor and Con watched in heavy silence as the line of mourners dwindled and the flames sunk into embers.

Con cleared his throat. "So you still intend to acknowledge her as the heir to Timberline?"

"She is the heir," Elinor said, her mind replaying the image of Lady Lliane and Tae's father holding hands in the clearing, married in the old manner.

"Yes, I know. But think what you are doing," he urged. "You are elevating a commoner of non-ascended blood to noble status. Every other lord, whether they have holdings in the marches or in Resa, will know what you have done here. And they will all hate you for it."

Elinor was silent for long moments. "Let them," she said. "It wouldn't be the first time."

Con blinked. "No, but as you said, this isn't the Academy anymore, Elinor."

"Not it is not," she said. "It's more important now." She was quiet for a moment. "The lords will never change. They think everything I do is an affront to them. Their vision is so limited, so focused only on themselves that, of course, they think this is only about them. But they're wrong. This has never been about them." She took a deep breath, taking in the clean air of Timberline and feeling it fill her lungs. "It was about Lida. It was about Tae. I did it for them. And I would do so again for any who would need it. If that is an affront to the lords, then so be it."

Fixing her with a long look, Con lowered his voice. "If the other lords cannot have your blood, then they will look to make Timberline bleed in your stead, Elinor."

"Not immediately," she replied. "Not openly. Piersym murdered another noble. He broke the First Covenant of the Ascended. And I know he is not alone in this treachery. As much as the nobles feel themselves above the law, none of them would truly wish to test the king. They will want to keep this quiet, and a direct attack on me or Timberline will only cause more attention they can ill afford."

"But they will come. Eventually, they will strike."

"Yes," Elinor said gently. "And that is why whatever will become of Timberline, it must be Tae's decision. I cannot make that choice for her. I can only promise that if she chooses that path, she will not fight alone."

From behind, Elinor heard Tae's voice. "Then that makes the choice an easy one, doesn't it?"

Up close now, Elinor saw just how badly the girl was hurt. She was pale and there were dark circles under her eyes, made even starker by the whiteness of her skin. She leaned heavily on a cane and one arm was cradled protectively over her wounded abdomen. Still, there was a bright intensity in her eyes that shone despite her condition.

Elinor looked the girl directly in the eyes. "My duty to the king will take me away from here. You will have many enemies, Tae. For now, they won't dare strike at you directly. But they will come for you. When that day comes, call for me. No matter how dire it may seem, just hold, and I will be here by your side. I promise you that."

Tae nodded, tears in her eyes. "I will not fail you, nor this gift you have given me."

Elinor embraced the girl, careful of her injuries. Then, she looked back at Con. "We have some time before we go, and we have the engineers and the crews. What would it take to train the villagers to help rebuild Last Dawn Keep?"

"Rebuild her? I suppose I could put some plans together," Con said, but his face fell. "But she'll never be as she was."

"I wouldn't be so sure of that, Journeyman Engineer. Timberline is sacred. It is the ancient seat of a power that shaped the world. It may still surprise you."

Con smiled. "You've done a good thing here, Elinor."

"I did not do it alone."

Con bowed his head slightly. "Still, I wish I could have been there when you faced those Earth Tyrants. Just for old times' sake. That must have truly been a sight to see."

Elinor was quiet for a moment, and then shrugged.

"I don't know. From the stories, I thought they would be bigger."

Follow the continuing stories of Elinor in Book 2, Broken Banners. Coming Soon.

Author's Note
Echoes of the Ascended, Books 1

Thank you so much for reading *A Reaper of Stone*.

Mark and I met more than twenty-five years ago, and inspired by all the great fantasy authors of our childhood, we wanted, more than anything, to tell our stories as well. To share them with others. With you.

It has been a long journey to finally get here. It hasn't been easy, but nothing worthwhile ever is.

We've got many more stories to tell in Aedaron. Our mission is to get one new story out to you every month.

Different characters. Different stories. But our same love for the world, characters, drama, and action that matter most to us.

We hope you'll come along for the ride.

– Check us out at gelineauandking.com
– Like us at facebook.com/gelineauandking
– Follow us on Twitter @gelineauandking

Or send us your best wishes via astral projection. Whatever your medium, we accept love in all its forms.

Hope to see you again soon.

Mark & Joe

PROLOGUE

THE BOY FELT IT BEFORE he saw it.

There was a chill feeling, different from the usual cold that filled the stone halls of the orphanage. That cold was familiar and simple. You felt it in your bones. You endured it by hovering closer to the kitchen fire before the matron caught you, or by sharing a blanket with your chosen brothers and sisters.

But this was different. This was a sharp edged cold. Like the glitter that came off the knife they used to kill the goats. Like the ice that sheathed the old tree outside and made the branches snap off. He did not feel this cold in his bones, but in his very soul. And it made him want to whimper with fear.

He had tried to keep quiet. Already many of the other orphans were angry at him. The dancers and jugglers had them clapping and laughing, a rare treat for the forgotten children housed here.

Until he had begun screaming and pointing at one of the performers.

He had ruined the show, and the embarrassed matron sent the children off to their dormitories immediately. Their anger was palpable, a terrible thing he felt all around, and he could hear harsh whispers up and down the halls of the old fortress that served as the orphanage. "Crazy is at it again," he heard. "The lunatic's seeing monsters again." He knew if not for his friends, he would have suffered that night.

His friends Elinor, Alys, Roan, and Kay had not been angry, though. They believed him. They comforted him, drawing him away from the performers and out of the room without a look back at the ruined entertainment. Elinor wrapped an arm around his shoulders as they walked and Roan stared daggers at the other orphans, defying their anger at his friend. Together, they returned to the dormitory and prepared for bed.

No, his friends had not been angry like the other children were. They never were. But he also knew they did not understand. Not truly. Even he began to doubt himself. Perhaps the cruel whispers from the other children were right, he thought.

Until tonight. Until he had seen the blackheart just an arm's length away from him and he screamed and screamed till his throat was raw. Where their hearts should have been, oily mud and black smoke oozed from their chests to cover their bodies. He had seen them three times before, but never up close like this.

Even now, in the small hours of the night when everyone in the large room was asleep, the boy remained awake. The fear of the shadowed juggler would not leave him, and behind his closed eyes, he pictured the horrible darkness moving over the man. The feeling crept over him more and more. The cold feeling. Sharp. Dangerous.

He finally could not stand it any longer. His eyes snapped open, and he looked across the darkened room, past the simple cots the orphans all slept on.

And he saw it.

The blackheart was in the room. The rolling, oily blackness spilled from its chest like blood from a wound, deeper even than the dark of the night. It stood across the room from him, looming over the foot of one girl's bed. The boy felt his heart pounding, and he longed to reach out to touch his friends, either to wake them to see what he saw or to wake himself from what must be a nightmare. But he was too frightened to move.

As he watched, the juggler's shape sloughed off, dropping to the floor like a discarded garment. In its place was something more horrifying. The head became longer and had no eyes, only a round mouth from which the boy could see wicked teeth. It craned a long, serpent like neck toward the sleeping child while reaching forward with ragged claws at the end of spindly arms. The thing bent down to feed, and the boy moaned with terror.

The long neck whipped impossibly around, turning its eyeless face toward the boy. It dropped to all fours and charged across the room.

For the second time that night the boy screamed himself raw.

***

Ferran opened his eyes and tried to still his breathing. The room was warm. All around him were men and women, wearing the earthy colors favored by the Order of Talan. Many of them had their exposed skin heavily tattooed with strange symbols and designs. But all of them looked on him with understanding eyes.

An old man stepped forward, leaning heavily on a cane. Dark stripes were inked onto his weathered and wrinkled face, contrasting with the bright white of his long beard. He stood before Ferran and watched as the young man drew deep breaths.

"What did you see?" the old man asked.

Ferran matched the old man's gaze and steadied himself. "My past," Ferran said.

The old man studied him for a long moment and then nodded once. He stepped out of the way and made a gesture. Across the length of the chamber, a heavy iron door swung open, to reveal the creature from his memory. The monstrous head whipped around and the circular maw

3

puckered at the air. Long talons scraped across the floor with a high pitched keening as it drew away from the open door.

"What do you see?" the old man asked from behind Ferran.

In his left hand, Ferran felt the weight of a long length of silver chain, and he let one end fall to the floor with a clear, bright ring. His other hand tightened around the haft of a short spear, the blade held before him, catching the light of the torches carried by the members of the Order who looked on.

"What do you see?" the old man asked once more.

Ferran's lips drew back into a savage smile. "My future," he said and advanced on the monster.

BEST LEFT IN THE SHADOWS

ACT 1
A MESSY LITTLE MURDER

The slow lapping of the Prion River mingled with the creaking wood symphony of the water wheel beside the dock. Moonlight tinted the heavy fog as the last hours of night became the first hours of morning. The heavy mist lay upon the woman's corpse, fat drops of dew sitting on the blood and making it shine.

Alys bent over the body, her hands on her hips as she studied the dead woman's face. Young. Roughed up. She may have been pretty once, but it was impossible to tell now. Old bruises and new mixed with dried blood to create a mask over the girl's features.

Alys turned to the man standing against the wooden wall of the pier and shrugged. "What do you want me to say?"

The man finished speaking to a pair of city guards and waited until the two men clanked away in their armored breastplates and shiny helms. His light hair, always cropped close and crisply perfect, shone briefly in the glow from the torches the guards carried. Alys caught just a glimpse of those familiar blue eyes before the light from the torches faded away.

He pulled his long coat closer about him against the chill of the morning. The black fabric and gray striping of a royal magistrate made him stand out.

She corrected her thoughts. *Stand out even more.*

"I want you to tell me what happened," he said.

She laughed, adjusting the large-bladed scythe that she carried across her back. "What happened? Someone killed her, Magistrate Inspector Daxton Ellis," Alys said, punctuating every syllable of the man's title with a clipped enunciation.

He gave her a long, hard stare. "Nothing is ever easy with you, is it, Alys?"

"It's part of my charm," she said, moving over to the wall beside him. As she drew closer, she studied his face – the subtle play of muscles around his eyes, the set of his mouth. He was always easy to read. "You know who she is." It was not a question.

He hesitated at first, then said, "She's Lydia Ashdown."

"Old name," she said.

"Old everything."

Alys shrugged. "Doesn't mean much down here in Lowside. You're sure it's her?"

The inspector gave her a slow nod. "She's been missing for three months now. The parents held out hope that she had just had a rebellious jaunt out to the marches to visit friends or relatives." He shook his head. "Still, the magistrates were given her description. We knew there was a chance we'd find her like this, but there was always hope. At least until tonight."

Alys flicked her tongue against her teeth in silent annoyance. "That doesn't answer my question, Dax. How do you know this is her?"

"When she was younger, she was playing and fell into the hearth," he said. "It left her with a burn scar between her..." He cleared his throat. "Over her heart area."

2

Alys laughed. "So you tore open this poor girl's bodice for your salacious gaze? Why Dax, you cad!"

"The mark is distinctive. It looks like a sparrow."

"A sparrow?" Alys said in disbelief, kneeling down and opening up the corpse's shirt. Underneath the clothing, on the stiff, waxy flesh was a brownish red mark. It sat between her breasts, just over her heart. To Alys's surprise, it actually did look quite a bit like a sparrow in flight. "Amazing. Highside even has prettier scars than we do."

"This is hardly a laughing matter, Alys. The Ashdowns are true blooded. They have a direct line to the First Ascended. And their daughter is dead. In Lowside."

"Ah," Alys said. "And there it is. I was wondering what had prompted the chief magistrate to assign you here, dear Dax. Now, I know. You true bloods stick together, right? They brought you in to tidy things up and make sure the Ashdown family is confident that a person of the correct breeding and background is investigating the death of their poor child."

His eyes narrowed. "I thought we weren't making this personal?" he remarked, an edge in his voice. "Wasn't that one of the rules?" He paused and shook his head. "I'm not here to tidy anything up. I am here for justice. To find who is responsible. It does not matter to me in the slightest how true hers or anyone's blood may be. You should know that most of all." He looked at her and in his eyes was that familiar look of resolution, but also a bit of challenge as well.

That was new.

Silently, she cursed him. As ever, he knew all the right buttons to push. And he was right. Those were the rules. Keep it business. Alys presented a charming smile to him. "A noble endeavor, Dax. And one I would be glad to assist you with, but you know that nothing is free, Magistrate Inspector. Especially down here in Lowside."

"The city will pay for your assistance. Discretely, of course."

"I don't need coin. I can steal whatever coin I want." He remained quiet at that, and she chuckled. "Oh come now, Daxton. Surely it hasn't been so long you can't remember what a girl really wants?"

"I can't do it. You know I can't." But even as he spoke, Alys saw his eyes move back to the body before them.

The way his attention kept returning to the corpse, the way his breath came a little faster as she was about to move away. This was a serious case. A Highside victim, old family nobility, found in Prionside. Dax was out of his element here and he knew it.

"What do you want to know?" he said at last.

Alys moved in closer and whispered in his ear. "The appointment for Justicar of the Second District is coming. I want to know who's going to get the nod for that post and what leverage the appointers have on them."

Dax spun away. "You're out of your damned mind."

"Oh, unclench. You know I will be discreet, Dax. I always am."

"It hasn't been fully decided yet," Dax said through tight lips.

Alys waggled a finger in front of him. "Stop trying to avoid it. This is no small endeavor you are asking me to join you on. And knowing who's getting tapped should just about cover it. The Second District Justicar is the law in Lowside." She paused and smiled at him. "Well, the king's law, anyway."

He did not smile back. If anything, his frown seemed to intensify. "It's not you that I don't trust, Alys. It's who you'll sell the information to."

"Believe me, Dax. They know the rules too," she said. "This is their world. One that they carved out for themselves and built with sweat and blood. They're not going to shit on all that."

Alys met his gaze with her own dark eyes. She saw him break first, unable to keep from looking at the corpse. Inside, she smiled.

"Fine. I will find out what you want, but I will want results first."

"Of course," she said.

She pressed her hand against her heart and then held it out to him. He did the same and they clasped forearms, sealing the deal.

"The Ashdowns will want someone to answer for this," Dax said. "They will look to the top and think that Blacktide Harry himself is involved," he said.

"No chance it's Harry," she said.

"He's still boss in Prionside District, right? The Stevedore Rats still answer to him?"

"Why Magistrate Inspector! It seems you have been keeping an ear to the ground in regards to the goings on of the shade folk."

"It's his domain," he said. "And he's got the reputation for violence."

"Oh Harry's as black-hearted a bastard as you'll ever meet, but he has no temper. Everything he does is cold. But even more, this," she said, pointing to the body of the young woman, "is bad for business. It's public. It shines a light on Prionside. The Blacktide would never do anything to disrupt business on the docks. Never."

"Well, then if he is so innocent, he shouldn't mind the inconvenience of a few questions, should he?" He fixed her with a look that slowly evolved into a smile. "You can arrange a meeting, can't you?"

"You're wasting time," Alys said, reaching back and adjusting the large scythe in its harness, and checking the daggers at her belt. "But I suppose, if you are set on it, it wouldn't hurt to pay him a visit anyway. If you really want to follow this, we'll need the Blacktide's blessing if we're going to be poking around Prionside."

With that, she offered him her arm. "Come along, Magistrate Inspector. It's late at night, and the streets can be so very dangerous," she said, batting her eyes at him. "An escort is ever so important."

Dax frowned again, but behind his eyes, Alys caught just the barest hint of amusement. "Then I suppose it is good that I have one," he said.

FAITH AND MOONLIGHT

ROAN

The smell of the fire still clung to the boy.

It clung to all of his friends as well, filling the space of the small wagon they slept in. In spite of the open top, in spite of the cold breeze that blew throughout the day, even in spite of the two weeks that had passed since the night the orphanage burned down, the children still carried the smell with them. The scent of soot and ashes, of fear and death.

The loss of the orphanage weighed on him more than he thought it would. It had not been much, but in the two years he had been there, it had been more of a home than he had ever known. It had been where he first met the others, and where they welcomed him in as family.

And now, they had all lost everything.

Roan slammed his hand against the wagon's side, the coarse-grained wood biting into his knuckles. In the cold, quiet of the late evening, the sound of it was like a crack of thunder, and immediately he regretted it.-

"Can't sleep?" Kay's dark brown eyes shined in the low light.

"Did I wake you?" he whispered.

"No," she said, rubbing her eyes sleepily as she sat up. Her long brown hair had fallen forward, obscuring her face. Her features were soft and pale, accentuated by large, bright eyes that seemed to take in everything at once. He had always thought she was beautiful.

"I did. I'm sorry, Kay," he said, keeping his voice low. "Go back to sleep."

"What's wrong?" she asked, shifting more upright, a slight edge of tension in her voice.

"Nothing. Just excitement, I guess. Cadell says we should arrive at Resa the day after tomorrow." He gestured toward the only adult in the wagon, the old man handling the reins of the mule team that pulled the wagon. The back of his bald head was wrinkled and marred with small scars and dark, tattooed lines.

Kay's eyes narrowed. "Do you really think we can trust him? That he's telling the truth about starting new lives there?" she asked. "I mean, after everything, how can we trust anything?"

"He did save our lives," he reminded her gently.

"And you saved his."

"Well, that means we should be able to trust each other, don't you think?"

Kay was quiet for a moment. "I guess so," she said, but there was no confidence in her words.

In the half-light, she looked smaller. Diminished. The suspicion and doubt in her voice hurt Roan in his heart. Kay had always seen the best in people. She had always been the first to smile. The first to trust.

But that was before the fire.

Roan reached out and Kay moved to sit beside him. She seemed so small as she settled in. He tousled her hair in an effort to try and cheer her. "Come on. There are great things ahead for us. We're going to become Razors. Like the great heroes in Elinor's stories."

The wagon rocked slowly and both looked to Elinor asleep on the floor, Alys and Ferran beside her. Roan felt a twinge of sadness at the thought of separating from his friends after they had been through so much.

Almost as if she could read his thoughts, Kay sighed. "I wish they could come with us," she whispered.

Roan slowly nodded. "Me too, but they won't be too far away. And they'll be following their dreams. Making them come true, just like we are."

"Are we, Roan?" Kay asked. "How? Other than kitchen chores, I've never held a blade in my life. How am I going to become some great warrior?"

"That's what the school is for," he chided her gently. "They'll handle teaching us and Cadell said he will give us a letter of introduction, so they will give us a chance. That chance is all we need."

Even as he spoke, he hated himself for lying. Kay was right. She had no experience fighting, and she would be going up against the best in the kingdom, students who trained their entire lives for that one sole purpose. She had little chance of making it. And if she didn't, if she failed, then she would truly have nothing.

But what choice did they have?

"What if I don't make it?" Kay said quietly.

"You will."

"How do you know that?"

"Because I'll make sure you do," he said. "I'll be there by your side."

There was a pleading look in her eyes. "And if we fail?"

His lips tight, Roan locked eyes with her. "Then we face whatever comes after. Together."

Kay found his hand and gripped it tightly with both hands. Roan squeezed back. She nodded softly, and then laid her head on his shoulder. He could hear her soft breathing and in a few moments, she was asleep again.

Despite her warmth, Roan felt cold.

His mind brought forth memories of childhood, of being on the ragged edge, fighting for every mouthful of food, desperation turning you into a wild, feral thing that was barely human. That had been life, until Kay and the others took him in. He could not allow her to fall into that existence. It would change her. It would break her. As he had seen it happen to so many others.

No. He couldn't let it come to that.

He wouldn't let it come to that.

She had saved him. Now, he would do the same for her.

He wrapped his arms around her and stayed perfectly still as she slept. The thud of the team's hoofbeats seemed to count down the moments remaining in their journey to Resa, the capital, and to the Razor School of Faith, where their new lives awaited.

A REAPER OF STONE

A Lady is dead. Her noble line ended. And the King's Reaper has come to reclaim her land and her home. In the marches of Aedaron, only one thing is for certain. All keeps of the old world must fall.

Elinor struggles to find her place in the new world. She once dreamed of great things. Of becoming a hero in the ways of the old world. But now she is a Reaper. And her duty is clear. Destroy the old. Herald the new.

"A classic fantasy tale with a strong, admirable heroine and a nice emotional punch. Great start to an enjoyable new series!"
— RL King, author of *The Alastair Stone Chronicles*

"A Reaper of Stone has the essence of a traditional fantasy epic, full of adventure and beautiful, lyrical prose, in well under a hundred pages."
— *Books by Proxy*

REND THE DARK

The great Ruins are gone. The titans. The behemoths. All banished to the Dark and nearly forgotten. But the cunning ones, the patient ones remain. They hide not in the cracks of the earth or in the shadows of the world. But inside us. Wearing our skin. Waiting. Watching.

Once haunted by visions of the world beyond, Ferran now wields that power to hunt the very monsters that he once feared. He is not alone. Others bear the same terrible burden. But Hunter or hunted, it makes no difference. Eventually, everything returns to the Dark.

"Atmospheric, fast paced, engaging quick read, with a satisfying story and glimpses of Supernatural *and King's* IT. *"*

– BooksChatter

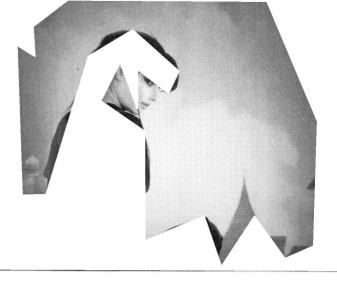

Best Left in the Shadows

A Highside girl. Beaten. Murdered. Her body found on a Lowside dock. A magistrate comes looking for answers. For justice.

Alys trades and sells secrets among the gangs and factions of Lowside. She is a daughter of the underworld. Bold. Cunning. Free. When an old lover asks for help, she agrees. For a price.

Together, they travel into the dark heart of the underworld in search of a killer.

"I was blown away by the detail and world building that was accomplished in so few pages. I didn't feel like I was seeing a section of a puzzle, more like I was reading a story that would contribute to a larger whole, but is compelling and rich all on its own."

— *Mama Reads, Hazel Sleeps*

FAITH AND MOONLIGHT

Roan and Kay are orphans.

A fire destroys their old life, but they have one chance to enter the School of Faith.

They are given one month to pass the entry trials, but as Roan excels and Kay fails, their devotion to each other is put to the test.

They swore they would face everything together, but when the stakes are losing the life they've always dreamed of, what will they do to stay together?

What won't they do?

"You can really feel Roan's desire and dream to be something more and you can also feel Kay's frustration and struggle. And underneath all that you can practically touch how much they care about each other."

— *White Sky Project*

Made in the USA
San Bernardino, CA
27 April 2019